# Girl Under The Christmas Tree

## A Steamy Holiday Romance Novella

### Cassandra O'Leary

Cassandra O'Leary

Cassandra O'Leary, Author

Melbourne, Australia

**cassandraolearyauthor.com**

# Blurb

## Girl Under The Christmas Tree

**A** hilarious holiday romance on the steamy side, featuring a girl who won't say no to a fling, a guy who needs some holiday fun, one naughty night in a hotel suite... and a conga line of Santas!

Yuki Yamimoto isn't the kind of girl to say no to opportunity, especially when it comes swaggering into the five-star hotel where she works, dressed in a three-piece suit. The handsome wavy haired man with a movie star smile and charming Irish accent is almost irresistible... If only he wasn't a hotel guest!

Declan Moriarty can't keep his eyes off the gorgeous girl at hotel Reception. Her wide eyes and flirting have him wondering, should he dare ask her out? When his whole life has fallen into the cosmic toilet the past year, it seems too much to ask for a dream girl like Yuki for Christmas. But maybe just this once, luck might be on his side.

A steamy Christmas Eve date has them both wanting more, but Yuki isn't supposed to fraternize with hotel guests. Not even a cheeky, handsome guest who also happens to be one of the youngest tech CEOs in Ireland. She definitely isn't supposed to stay in his hotel suite, even if it is just a fling for one night only. What if she loses her Christmas bonus or gets fired?

Declan wants nothing more than to keep Yuki, the girl under his Christmas tree. But he only has days in Melbourne, Australia before he has to fly back to Ireland for Christmas, then back to work. Is it foolish to risk putting his heart on the line again, when it was recently battered and bruised by his cheating ex-fiancée?

Yuki's about to embark on a life full of adventure...but will she get to keep Declan as part of the package deal? She hopes so. It's her number one Christmas wish.

# Author's Note

D ear reader,

This story is a prequel of sorts
or 'origin story' and companion piece to
my debut novel, *Girl on a Plane*, first
published by HarperCollins UK in 2016.

I loved re-visiting the minor character
of Yuki, back before she became a flight
attendant with Mermaid Airlines. I've
given her a fun backstory with plenty of
romance.

*Girl Under The Christmas Tree* has a happy for now (HFN) ending, leaving Yuki's future wide open. I may have to write another spin off story like this!

Happy reading,
*Cassandra x*

# Contents

# Chapter One

## The Palladian Hotel, Melbourne, Australia

**A few years ago...**

Yuki wasn't the type of girl to say no to opportunity when it came knocking, or even when it came swaggering into the five-star hotel reception area dressed in a crumpled three-piece suit. God, how she was a sucker for a man in a tailored three-piece suit.

She'd nabbed the best spot in the foyer, a cushy seat under the hotel's ginormous Christmas tree, which was covered in sparkly lights and glass ornaments. She was busy staring into space, about to scoff a Christmas cookie and a cafe latte in a reusable cup, when she spotted him coming her way. Since she was on a break, she wasn't quite prepared to be questioned by the man.

He cleared his throat, and she glanced at him, then did an actual, cartoon style, double take when she saw his face. *Handsome stranger alert...*

"Excuse me, but I was wondering if you could point me in the direction of the Grand Ballroom. I found a big room over there," he gestured over his shoulder, "but it isn't particularly grand."

*Oh. My. God.* He was Irish. The devastating charm Irish men had in spades, was her personal Kryptonite. Everyone knew it. The way he said the word *grand* made her want to bite her tongue before she accidentally swallowed it. And there was more.

She let her gaze travel all the way up the full height of him, to take in the kind of perfect face that made her wish she could draw portraits. His eyes were incredibly blue and sparkly, and contrasted with his wavy hair, a kind of mahogany, almost black with a hint of warm red. *Assessment: very attractive.* Strong jaw, a little dark stubble, nice large hands. He held a leather briefcase in front of him, and she was staring at his hands like a weirdo hand stalker.

He smiled and she almost cried. His teeth were perfect, like movie star teeth. Did real people have smiles that lit up a room like a string of high wattage Christmas tree lights? Apparently, yes.

If she had been standing behind the reception desk she would have been more polished, more professional. Probably less pouty. She'd only wanted to have her cookie and eat it too! Was that too much to ask? Apparently. But she wanted to talk to him now. A lot.

Yuki smiled, putting a little extra sweetness into it, looking up at him from under her eyelashes. She carefully put her cookie back in its little paper bag and brushed powdered sugar off her fingers. "Oh, that's the Federation Room. Not quite so grand. I can show you the way, if you like? It's a little tricky to navigate the mezzanine level."

"That's kind of you. But I wouldn't want to interrupt your coffee break, Miss—"

"Yuki. You can call me Yuki. And it's no problem, sir. I was just about to go and see the Events Manager up that way." That was a lie, but an innocent one. Her friend Melanie was in charge of events at the hotel, and she'd need to tell her all about this man. They always alerted each other to the hot guests, purely for ogling purposes. Being overly friendly or dating the guests was *verboten* by their stricty-pants German hotel manager, Mr Heyer.

"Ah, well. In that case I'd be delighted to have a guide, Miss Yuki. I'm Declan, by the way. Declan Moriarty." He extended his right hand, and she could have fainted with shock. Guests didn't shake hands with staff. But she took his hand, because of course she wanted to touch him.

It was a mistake because he was too sexy. She reached out and shook his hand, or rather he enveloped her small hand totally in his grasp. The heat of his skin was startling, and she bit the inside of her lip to stop a gasp escaping. Tiny ripples of some mysterious energy passed between them, heating her skin and sending prickles of awareness through her whole body. Like static electricity. It certainly felt like every hair on her body was standing on end.

Yuki shivered, although it was far from cold in the Aussie summer. "Mr Moriarty."

He gripped her hand and pumped it a couple more times, grinning at her like the Cheshire cat. "You can call me Declan".

"Declan." She nodded, feeling like Alice descending into another world, a backwards world where up was down, as her stomach had dropped through a virtual rabbit hole.

She let go of his hand and stuffed her
cookie in her purse. "Please, follow me."

The girl called Yuki, a stunning wee lass,
rose from her chair under the Christmas
tree. She had been sitting there serene as
a princess, or an angel, lit up and shining
with a silvery glow about her. Declan had
been drawn to her, couldn't resist talking
to her.

Now she walked away from him at an
impressive pace for someone in a skinny
dress and heels. He almost yelled at her
to slow down, but then...he might have
scared her. He was a hotel guest after all,
and she worked there. Just trying to do her
job.

Her little black dress with the white
accents told him she was staff, though he

had been at the hotel a few days and hadn't seen her around before. She wiggled her way through the foyer and he stared after her for a few moments, then half-jogged to catch up. He shouldn't flirt or banter with her. No, definitely not. Pretty as she was...

She stopped and flicked her long shiny black ponytail over her shoulder, glancing his way. "Are you coming, sir?"

Oh, but those words out of her pretty lips were a temptation to play. "Yuki, my dear. I'm simply admiring your athleticism. You practically hurdled that chair to get away from me." Not flirting at all. "Give a poor, short legged Irish man a chance." He pressed his hand to his heart.

Her lips twitched. "Short legged? You have about half a metre on me."

He shrugged. "True, but I don't have your gazelle-like grace. Or would you prefer, a flamingo?"

This time she did giggle. The sound was delightful. "Your laugh is like heavenly music". He crossed the floor to catch up to her.

"Um, thank you." She shook her head. "This way." She gestured to a small ramp and a flight of stairs tucked away in a corner.

They walked up the stairs, Yuki ahead of him. "I haven't stayed in this hotel before, but I think I like it more than the Sydney hotel."

"Really? The Sydney Harbour views are amazing though. Well, I think so."

Declan nodded, pausing at the landing where she'd stopped. "Melbourne is my favourite place in Australia though. It's not just the coffee, to be fair, Dublin has good coffee too. I like the people here. More friendly. Genuine."

Yuki beamed at him. "That's exactly what I think. But don't tell my manager. He used to run the Sydney hotel." Yuki continued up the stairs, and he followed.

"Is that so?" He'd met Mr Heyer and hadn't been blown away by his friendliness. He talked down to his staff, and that was something Declan couldn't abide.

A minute later, Yuki directed him to the Grand Ballroom, at the top of the stairs and to the right, through a large sunlit atrium. "I'll be on the reception desk this afternoon if you need anything else, sir."

"Thanks again. And it's Declan."

"Right. See you later, Declan." She ducked her head, and he could have sworn he saw a hint of blush cross her cheek.

The delightful Yuki would be at reception? Then he'd be sure to pay her a visit. He watched her walk away, swaying as she went in her snug little dress. Great legs, even better arse. Petite, and pretty. So very pretty.

"Melanie?" Yuki skidded round the corner into the events office and knocked on her friend's office door. "Mel?"

The door opened, but Melanie had a phone plastered to her ear and pressed her index finger to her lips, signally for Yuki to hush.

"Yes, absolutely. I'll confirm the seating arrangements with the dinner crew and let you know." Melanie gestured for Yuki to come in and sit down. "Okay, thanks very much."

She ended the call and sat on the edge of her desk.

Melanie tossed her brown curly hair back and her face positively glowed. "Charity dinner dance for three hundred all confirmed for New Year's Eve. Yes!" She punched the air, then smiled so wide she was almost as toothy as Declan. Almost. "Nailed it, my friend. Now what's going on with you?"

"Um...phew." Yuki crossed her legs in the aqua armchair in the corner of the office, then fanned her face with her hand. She was a little warm, no denying it. "I just met probably the most handsome man on the face of the earth, he shook my hand, and now I'm sweating."

Melanie raised a perfectly arched eyebrow. "Well now. Details please."

Yuki groaned. "He's a guest! Declan Moriarty... Dark wavy hair, eyes like the Pacific Ocean, tall and with this gorgeous smile."

Melanie nodded. "Oooooh. Good, good. He's with the IT conference that's here this week. He owns a hot new start-up. One of the youngest CEOs here, apparently. Not ideal he's a guest, but never mind."

Yuki leaned forward, whispering the most important fact. "And he's Irish!"

Melanie gasped, then covered her mouth with her hand. "Oh no. Did you pee your pants when he spoke to you?"

Yuki rolled her eyes. "Shut up! Okay, nearly. His accent is just soooo cute!"

Giggling, Melanie stood and waggled her finger at Yuki. Dressed in her severe grey suit, she looked like a school headmistress except for her wild curls, bouncing as she moved. "Yuki Yamimoto, I demand that you flirt with this man, and have some actual fun. You've been far too down in the dumps lately."

Yuki sighed, then opened her purse and found her cookie, and unwrapped it. "I know. It's because I'm waiting to find out about that job. It's been a whole month." She jammed the cookie in her mouth and ate it in two bites.

"I know, the flight attendant job would be awesome, even though I'd miss you. But you can't put your whole life on hold, waiting, just in case you get it."

Yuki finished chewing. "You're right. I know you're right. I can't seem to help wanting things I can't have."

Melanie sighed now and sat next to her on the arm of Yuki's chair. "You can have anything you want. You're young, beautiful..." Yuki snorted. "You are beautiful, believe me, Miss Hottie McTottie. More importantly, you're smart. Opportunity will come, and you'll be ready. But in the meantime..."

"Have some fun." She nodded. It was good advice. Melanie was wise, and more experienced than Yuki, in terms of men and life in general. Not to mention, she had a proper career.

Yuki wanted adventure, a life full of excitement. Maybe meeting Declan was a sign of good things coming her way.

"By the way," Melanie said with a teasing note in her voice, "Mr Meyer won't be here for the rest of this week. I heard he'll be in Sydney until after Christmas. If you were to say, flirt with a guest, he wouldn't even know. If you happened to go out with a certain Irishman, what's the worst that could happen?"

Yuki bit her lip. Right. She had a new Christmas wish list and Declan Moriarty was right at the top.

# Chapter Two

## Grand Ballroom, The Palladian Hotel

The keynote speaker on IT security was a shockingly boring American man, droning on for hours about denial of service attacks and hacking, which was a potentially interesting topic. He cracked a 'joke' about back-door entry being kind of sexy, and it was all Declan could do to stop himself heckling the man, to tell him to get the hell off the stage, like he was at a comedy club. But he needn't have bothered when the entertainment came busting in the door, uninvited.

A noise like...sleigh bells rang out, and Declan turned his head along with hundreds of other delegates. Searching for the source of the jingling, not to mention doors banging, he craned his neck to check out the ballroom's side doors, standing wide open. He saw a flash of red, a white beard, and yes, it certainly looked like Santa Claus.

"Ho, ho, ho!" A booming voice rang out. It sounded like Santa Claus, too. What was going on?

Declan stood, ignoring the frowns from a sea of men and women in grey and navy suits, and he pushed his way through the row of seats and out into the aisle. The seats were set up theatre style, and he could easily escape through a side door near the coffee station. Striding out of the ballroom door, he stopped in his tracks at a ridiculous sight.

Santa sat in one corner of the large space, on a golden throne no less. A pile of presents sat beside him, along with Mrs Claus and a few elves in full costumes. A photographer had set up his equipment for photos with Santa, complete with North Pole signs. So IT conference delegates could have a photo with Santa on their tea break? That wasn't even the most ridiculous thing.

He stuck out his hand, blinked several times, not quite believing what he saw. Tiny flakes of white fluttered through the air. Cold, damp flakes. It was snowing in the atrium. Inside the hotel. In Australia. In December. Peak summer, in other words. His mouth popped open, and he craned his neck upwards. A snow machine?

He turned round in a circle, staring at the white flakes falling, swirling around him. When he lowered his gaze, he saw Yuki across the large space, spinning in a circle. Her eyes were wide, and she had that joyful expression, a look of wonder, he remembered from Christmas when he was a child.

Without fully realising what he was doing, his feet were in motion and he walked towards her. He found himself face to face with Yuki. Well, she was still a few metres away, but her gaze found his and they connected. He couldn't describe it any other way. Her eyes lit up and her smile spread into a full-fledged grin, and something inside him melted.

He hadn't seen her yesterday afternoon, hadn't had a spare minute between conference sessions and meetings in the Melbourne city office. When he dropped by Reception in the late evening, she wasn't on duty. He ended up asking for extra pillows and went to bed. After two glasses of whiskey and a hot shower, he managed to sleep. And he had dreamed about a petite, raven haired beauty.

"Isn't this amazing?" Yuki whispered, as if it was a secret. She had come right up to stand beside him, close enough for him to breathe in the scent of her hair, a floral concoction with a hint of coconut. She smelled like a tropical vacation, which was exactly what he needed.

He let his mouth stretch out in a grin. "Aye. Amazing." His gaze drifted to her lips, until she blinked and looked away. He cleared his throat. "But I have to wonder, what about all this slush? It can't be good for the carpet." He lifted his feet, one at a time, inspecting the soles of his now damp leather shoes.

Yuki glanced his way, then around the room. "Oh, that's not good. I doubt if the Events team approved this. I wonder if my friend Melanie knows..."

"Oh no!" A tall, curly haired woman in a grey suit shouted, then screeched to a halt after coming hard around the corner into the space. She pointed up at the snow, then across the room at a certain jolly fella in a red suit. "You! I never agreed to this!" She marched towards the head Santa sitting on his throne. He was clearly on her naughty list.

Yuki stared at her, then glanced at Declan with a crinkle of worry on her forehead. "Um, I think she knows now. This could get ugly." She flipped her ponytail over her shoulder and whispered, "Let's get out of here."

Glancing at her familiar little black dress, he asked, "Aren't you working?"

She shook her head. "I already clocked off for today." Yuki bit her lip, and she was a perfect mix of sweet and tempting. Nervous though, if he was guessing.

He didn't need to be asked twice. "After you." He gestured for her to take the lead, and he followed Yuki, sidestepping piles of wrapped presents in one corner.

They made their way to the nearest elevator. Yuki pressed the Down button, and they stood waiting in silence. Well, the woman he assumed was Melanie was shouting about contacts and property damage in the background, while *All I Want For Christmas Is You* played cheerily on through the sound system. But he and Yuki didn't say a word, just shared a look that was half silent laughter, half confusion. She pressed her lips together, he cleared his throat and hummed along with the song.

The elevator doors opened with a *ping*, and they both stepped in, keeping a careful few paces distance. There were two other people in the car, one staff member from housekeeping, the other a guest in touristy shorts and t-shirt. Yuki politely nodded to the guest and said, "Good afternoon."

Declan didn't know why exactly, but he kept his mouth firmly closed. Yuki was different with other people around, more reserved. This may not have meant anything, but to him it was a sign. She was interested in him. Probably. He hoped so.

He chanced a sideways look at her, and she was watching the lights of the elevator's display change from M for Mezzanine, to R for Reception. The doors opened and the other two people got out.

When the doors closed again, Yuki turned his way and smiled, her cheeks touched with pink. She spoke softly, keeping her eyes on him. "I was going to ask Melanie if she wanted to come with me to a Christmas market. I don't suppose you would—"

"I'd love to."

"Oh, good." She licked her lower lip with the tip of her tongue and he almost had an aneurysm.

His face heated, he lost his train of thought. Was there a word for awkward anticipation? *Awkipation*? He was bursting full of it.

The elevator light changed to LG for Lower Ground floor, and she stepped forward, so he placed his hand in the small of her back, just for a moment. Yuki's soft inhale of breath was music to his affection-deprived ears. How long had it been since a woman wanted to spend time with him, to hang out? Too long.

They headed out to the street, together. And he thanked his lucky stars.

## Christmas Market

## Southbank, Melbourne

Yuki didn't know if she'd lost her mind, or if she'd finally found her dating mojo once and for all. She had asked out a man, a deliciously sexy man, and he'd come with her. Just like that!

They walked side by side along the south bank of the Yarra River, the sun sparkling on the water giving it a magical look, not the murky brown river of sludge on show in winter. A river cruise boat floated by, filled with people dressed in fancy clothes, drinking champagne. An office Christmas party, probably.

Skyscrapers of the city centre and the stunning older buildings like Flinders Street Station were just across the water, but here it was Christmas land. Market stalls lined one side of the pedestrian pathway, baubles and sprigs of pine tree hung from lamp posts. Families and couples wandered through the market, picking up handmade gifts and eating treats from other stalls and food trucks. The sound of festive songs played by a brass band, floated on the breeze from the other end of the market.

Declan sighed, a satisfied sound that made her want to ask him what he was thinking, or kiss him. "This is a pretty spot,

Miss Yuki. I like Melbourne. It reminds me of Dublin, to be honest. But the weather is better here, of course."

Yuki giggled like a school girl. This man affected like that, she felt lighter, carefree. "The weather in Melbourne is revolting most of the year. Rainy drizzle, freezing cold wind and grey skies."

"It really is like Dublin, then."

She snort-laughed this time, and she would have been embarrassed except he grinned, his whole face lighting up. He also took her arm in an old-fashioned gentlemanly way. The way it made her feel wasn't so innocent. Her whole body heated—the sun had nothing on the way Declan had her glowing.

Yuki kept walking and caught a glance of a popular stall. "Oh, look at the crystals over there." They steered through a bunch of people to take a closer look at a stall filled with glittering jewels, Swarovski crystals and semi-precious stones.

The jewellery wasn't too expensive, but so pretty that she ooohed and aahhed over more than one piece. She touched a string of transparent crystals with a large silver pendant at the end. "It's gorgeous, but I couldn't possibly justify it." Very sensible. She was trying to save money after all. But it was sad to leave it there, unloved and unbought.

"Wrap it up, please." Declan's voice was deep and sure from her left side. She turned to him, mouth agape. "You can't just go around buying me necklaces, willy nilly!"

His lips tipped up at the corners. "Willy nilly? Aye, I think you'll find I can, even higgeldy piggeldy. Consider it an early Christmas gift." He winked at the older woman who ran the stall, a stunning silk headscarf wrapped around her head. "I'll have one of these bracelets for my Mam too."

The stall holder wrapped his purchases and offered her holiday wishes, and Yuki stood there like she'd been frozen to the spot. Buying her presents? Already? In the same breath as buying things for his mother...this could be something. Something real. Maybe.

She sneakily looked at him side-on while he chatted away in that oh-so-charming accent. He was too good to be true. She took a sip from her water bottle, biding her time while her mind performed triple backflip gymnastics.

He was from another country. He'd be leaving soon. Anyway, he probably didn't even fancy her. He was only being polite. She couldn't go falling for him...

Declan handed her the little parcel, and murmured, right near her ear, "Here, Miss Yuki. A little something to stuff in your stocking."

She laughed, and choked. Water exploded from her lips. The horror! She ducked her head, but Declan moved closer, touching her lips with his fingertip. She tipped her head up to meet his eyes, and there was A Moment. His thumb brushed her lower lip, wiping off drops of water, and she could have sworn her heart stopped.

"There now." Declan cleared his throat and stepped away from her. "Right. Right! Should we get something to eat?"

Oh no. Had she scared him off with her sheer silliness?

*Oh, give me strength.* Declan raised his eyes to invisible higher powers, and wished for the billionth time he was as smooth as Cary Grant in an old movie. Then again, Cary did do a few bumbling comedy scenes, and women still liked him, so maybe all hope wasn't lost. And his real name was Archibald, a million times worse than Declan.

They walked through the crowd of shoppers, Yuki to his right. She'd gone quiet. He didn't know what to make of it. It was not his usual style to hit on women he'd only just met. Not at all.

When he'd met Kendra, his ex, his first thought was, nice woman, capable, she probably wouldn't pressure him to be romantic. They worked together, and they got along fine. They didn't go on a real date for at least a month. Now that he thought about it, that wasn't a good sign. Looking back, their relationship was probably doomed. There was never a real spark.

Looking at Yuki, there were sparks enough to set off a spectacular New Year's Eve fireworks show.

"What about a taco?" Yuki had stopped walking and was staring at the chalkboard menu outside a food truck. The whole space was decorated with fairy lights and strings of silver stars, fully pimped-out for the holiday season.

"Sure, sounds good." Declan ordered a taco with interesting local ingredients – Barramundi fish and lemon myrtle mayo, who knew that was a thing? – with an Aussie beer on the side. He carried his and Yuki's drinks and found them a table on the tiny lawn by the riverside.

When she sat beside him, instead of opposite, he couldn't think for a few

seconds. This was a date now, right? He
was almost sure. He undid the first two
buttons of his shirt and rolled up his
sleeves. He was hotly aware of Yuki's eyes
on him as he moved.

She breathed out, then quickly said,
"This is the best date I've been on in ages."
She paused, then laughed lightly. "Was that
a weird thing to say?"

His laugh came out of nowhere, right
from his gut. "Ha! I don't think so, but
I'm hardly an arbiter of normal-ness. I am
a tech nerd. I rarely leave my cave."

Yuki tipped her head to one side,
studying his face. "I don't think that's true.
You own a company, right? I'm sure you
get out and about. Women are probably
falling all over you, looking like..." She
waved her hand vaguely in front of him,
gesturing from his head to toes.

He tried not to scrunch up his face into a frown, but probably failed. "Looking like what exactly? An Irish hipster doofus?"

Her laugh caught him off guard, like a peal of silver bells. "No, you dag. I meant, all handsome and gorgeous. Full of Irish charm too."

His face nearly split in half from the stupid grin no doubt taking over his face. She thought he was handsome and gorgeous. And charming? Well, his luck definitely was changing. "Coming from a stunningly gorgeous girl, such as yourself, I'll take that as a huge compliment."

Now Yuki ducked and hid her face from him, looking out across the river at the city view. But he spotted the corner of her smile, the little dimple in her cheek. "But do you have women falling all over you? I've been burned before by men who pretended to be single. Especially when they're on holidays."

He nodded. Men could be arseholes, it was undoubtedly true. "Ah, I'm definitely single. I was engaged, but it ended over six months ago. Kendra and I didn't gel as a couple. Unfortunately, I have to see her tomorrow. She works at our Melbourne office now."

When Yuki turned back to meet his eyes, she looked worried. An adorable little line had formed in the spot between her eyebrows. "You broke off your engagement? What happened?"

His so-called friend had happened. Matthias was never blackening his doorstep again, after his part in ending Declan's relationship and leading their business down the wrong path.

He shrugged. That part of his life was over, so no harm talking about it. "Kendra wasn't quite as committed to the idea of monogamy as I was. Plus, my former friend and business partner was apparently better for her than I was, since I'm so old fashioned and stuck in my ways, insisting on complete honesty."

"Wow."

"Yeah. It is what it is. But I could have done without seeing my friend shagging my fiancée in my bed, two days before my wedding."

Yuki gritted her teeth, then plonked her beer down hard on the table. "What complete arseholes. I'd say you're better off without either of them."

"My thoughts exactly." Declan took a long swig of his beer. He never talked about that whole disaster, let alone to someone he'd only just met. But it felt good to get it out there, with Yuki.

A waitress arrived with their tacos, and as they ate they made small talk, no more heavy stuff. Decan's mind ticked over. He had to decide what to do.

Yuki was a real temptation. But was he ready to open himself up again with a woman? Kendra had ripped him right open with her style of makeshift open-heart surgery. He'd only just managed to stitch himself together.

He glanced across at Yuki to find her monstering a taco and licking her lips. "Oh. My. God. This taco is amaaaazing."

She licked her lips again, and he groaned before he could stop himself. "What?"

She was completely oblivious to how sexy she was. He shook his head. "Nothing. Enjoy your taco. I have to get back to the hotel. Work to do." He stood too quickly, awkward as hell, bumping his knee on the table leg.

"Oh. Will I see you tomorrow?"

His first instinct was to say no, to say goodbye to her. But his instincts sucked lately. He'd have to give it some thought. "Maybe. I have the office Christmas party, but I'll be around later."

Yuki smiled, a ray of sunshine. "Great. I'll be at Reception if you need me."

He waved and walked away, not sure if the lightness in his body was simply because of Yuki, or the odd feeling of being free to do what he wanted for a change. Probably both. He'd definitely give it some thought.

# Chapter Three

## The Palladian Hotel

For the past two days, Yuki's favourite guest had been flirting and hitting her with his high-beam super-smile in between his business meetings. Declan was making her wish for things that until a few days ago, seemed impossible.

Now he wandered into the hotel and he looked completely worn out. His rumpled wavy dark hair and scowl said his company's Christmas party hadn't been at all joyful. Poor Declan.

Tapping her foot where she stood behind the hotel reception desk in her low-heeled pumps, she sighed. Hotel guests were off limits to staff fraternizing. It was a crying shame, because she could see herself fraternizing all over him, in a naughty way. She should say no, if Declan flirted with her again or if he actually asked her out. He had been in fine form earlier, calling her "an afternoon delight" and "the angel of hotel reception".

Declan was obviously rich, handsome in a cheeky, wavy haired, blue eyed, wide shouldered kind of way, like a male model who dabbled in professional rugby and maybe romantic poetry. Smart as a whip, too. He was completely out of her league, not to mention one hundred percent off limits.

Still, she couldn't deny his delicious Irish accent had her melting into a puddle whenever he opened his mouth. Long story short, he was someone she should treat with deference, respect and absolutely not spill her overflowing store of bubbling lust over him. She could lose her job.

He sauntered up to the desk, taking his sweet time, grinning at her like a sexy loon when he spotted her watching him. Honestly, he was making it difficult to be good. Yuki tapped her fingertips on the desk. Only good little hotel staffers got Christmas bonuses. She would need the money when she (fingers crossed) moved to London in the new year.

On the other hand, she had to remember, she was no longer the type of girl to say no at all, as of exactly a week ago. Yuki had decided to lead a more adventurous life. To follow her heart, to listen to the inner voice that was whispering to her to take more chances, to expand her horizons...and to get properly laid. She would say yes, to every opportunity.

She forced her eyes away from him and pretended to check some bookings on the computer monitor.

"Good evening, Mr Moriarty," she began, and flicked her eyes up to meet his, a good six inches above her own. He was standing very close, leaning right up against the marble countertop. She sucked in a breath at the expression in his sapphire blue eyes. There was an unspoken challenge there, and undeniable heat.

"Good evening yourself, Miss Yuki. Now what would a gorgeous girl such as yourself be doing working on the eve of Christmas Eve?"

She kept her voice low. "Oh, you know. Working for The Man, earning my Christmas bonus." She bit her lip to stop herself talking. No way did he know what it was like, working for The Man. He was The Man. His tech company was one of the most successful start-ups in Ireland, or so she'd read. She now knew he had an Asia Pacific office in Melbourne too. He was only twenty-seven and had a staff of over one hundred people.

He raised one dark eyebrow, somehow setting his eyes to extra sparkly mode. "Ah, is that so? I wouldn't want to stand between a woman and her Christmas bonus. That could be bad. Cursed. It would be worse than breaking up a wedding, which I've had occasion to do, would you believe?"

Yuki pressed her lips together since she was in danger of giggling. "Ignore me, please. It's been a long week. The national department store Santa convention is in town and they drink a surprising amount of egg nog and whiskey, even at the breakfast buffet."

Her colleague, Carlos, snorted from where he stood at the bag check in area, a couple of metres away. He muttered something like, "True dat." She turned and gave him her best evil-eyed look. Carlos shook his head and backed away, ready to go on his break.

Yuki smiled at Declan, giving her handsome guest her full attention again. "My apologies, sir. What can I do for you this evening?"

The question apparently amused him. He flashed her a winning smile, all the more adorable because of the slightest gap between his front teeth. "To be honest, Yuki, my Christmas eve-eve plans have rather fallen flat. I was hoping you could recommend a good Irish pub or Australian type drinking establishment not too far away. I'd prefer no egg nog if at all possible."

She tapped at her computer screen. Angling it to show him some photos, she said, "Many of our guests like the Kookaburra Klub, only a block away."

He tilted his head, studying the photos. "Ah, bless. There's fake Kookaburras on the walls. No, I was thinking of a place you might personally recommend. Maybe somewhere you'd go after work."

Yuki nodded, catching his eye. She thought she'd caught his meaning too. "Let's see. When I finish work around midnight, like tonight, I sometimes Uber it to St Kilda and go to the Wheel and Barrow. It's a proper pub, beer on tap, live music, all that. Some friends of mine are in a band. They're playing tonight. Hard Candy."

She'd put it out there, sneakily dropped a big old hint that she'd be there later, and he could join her if he wanted to. No problem if he didn't mean what she thought he'd meant. She'd just sulk into her artisan pilsner and listen to the band.

"Thank you, Ms Yuki. I might change out of this cursed suit and head out there soon." He nodded, loosened his burgundy silk tie, and stared at her for a good half a minute. He hesitated, mouth open as if he was about to say something important. "Grand. Have a good night."

"Good evening, sir."

Yuki took a deep breath and watched him walk away, towards the bank of elevators on the east side of the hotel.

Right. She checked the time on her computer. It was already after eleven P.M.

Not long until her shift was over. She exhaled and pressed a hand to her chest. Her heart was going a mile a minute, and all he'd done was talk to her.

She would have to pace herself or she might pass out before the clock ticked over to midnight. Christmas Eve.

Declan ended the phone call after about forty long minutes and tossed his phone on the bed. He hadn't needed that call. Not now, not tonight. He scrubbed his hands through his hair, pacing his hotel suite like a trapped tiger in a cage.

Jon was a trustworthy man. His new second-in-command in the Irish office was both a lawyer and a systems architect. If Jon said the company had invested in the wrong technology and was sinking, Declan believed him. They had better patch the hole in the ship's hull or otherwise get a whole lot of life preservers. They would work out a plan, a new direction.

But first, he had a date. At least he thought so. Damn, was he really doing this?

Declan searched through his suitcase and the wardrobe in his hotel suite, looking for something to wear that wouldn't make him look like an absolute tool. All business clothes. "Bloody stupid. Suits should be banned," he muttered as he pulled out the drawers in the bureau.

He couldn't go to a local pub dressed like a typical IT guy, or he may as well wear a 'Kick Me' sign. But wait...his old friend Gabriel had given him a surf brand shirt when they'd caught up at Bells Beach last week. With his black jeans and trainers, that would do.

He quickly showered and changed, leaving his hair damp to curl as it pleased. Would Yuki like him this way? Out of his usual corporate uniform? She'd been in uniform all week, just like him.

Yuki, the gorgeous girl at the hotel's front desk. So friendly, so sweet. Her slight Australian accent, her long elegant neck with the little silver necklace she wore, and shiny hair black as midnight, always up in a sleek ponytail. Mostly it was her stunning wide eyes that had him almost lost for words. That wasn't like him at all. His old man often said Declan could talk the hind legs off a donkey. She had been the ultimate distraction from his business in Melbourne this week. And he definitely needed a distraction.

His ex-fiancée Kendra might have been a smart woman, a brilliant programmer, but as Chief Operating Officer she'd run the Asia Pacific arm of the company into the ground. He'd had to reassign her to another project, and he couldn't pretend it was a promotion. Hell of a way to ruin the office Christmas party, making that little announcement.

He'd got out of there as soon as possible, wishing Kendra well on his way out, though it half-killed him to do it. He could still feel the way she'd glared daggers at his back. He had more than enough anger to fire back at her if he chose. She'd been the one to cheat on him after all. He'd dodged a bullet there.

He nodded at his reflection in the bathroom mirror, running his fingers over the rough stubble along his jaw. "You can do this. Flirt with a pretty girl. Drink a few beers. Have a laugh. Pretend that the universe doesn't hate you, and your whole life didn't fall in the cosmic toilet this year."

He grabbed his phone and wallet, and headed out of the hotel, into the humid summer night to meet his taxi. And to meet the unlikely girl who had taken hold of his imagination, even his dreams.

Why did he have a feeling he was about to do something monumentally stupid? Ah well, it wouldn't be the first time.

# Chapter Four

## The Wheel & Barrow Pub, Melbourne

**Early hours of Christmas Eve**

Yuki stared into her beer, watching the swirl of foam on the surface and trying to find pictures in it, as if she was reading tea leaves in a porcelain cup. The beer wasn't even cold anymore. She wouldn't drink it warm, like an Englishman, or a psycho.

She blocked out the noise of punters arguing at the bar, and the frenetic thud of drums from the warm-up band. She settled back in the Reserved booth seat she'd found near the back of the band room. There was a silver Christmas tree balanced on the top of the booth, and she watched the string of lights wrapped around it flicker in pretty patterns.

She had hurried here from the hotel, thinking Declan Moriarty would be waiting for her. But obviously she was wrong. Clearly he'd changed his mind, or had a better offer. Hopefully it wasn't his ex keeping him busy.

She blocked out that depressing line of thought. Her friend's band would be on stage soon, and maybe one or two of her hotel co-workers would turn up too. The night didn't have to be a total write-off.

"Hello, Miss Yuki." The deep voice, the delectable Irish accent made her gasp. She flicked her head around to where he stood, just to her right.

"If it isn't the most beautiful girl in the world sitting under a Christmas tree. You must be waiting for Santa Claus. Will I do for company in the meantime?" He grinned, and even in the low lighting, his teeth almost glowed white.

Yuki's cheek muscles stretched out in a smile she couldn't contain. "You'll do. Get over here. I mean, please sit down, Mr Moriarty. Sir." She giggled like a fool. She couldn't help it. He came!

He shuffled into the booth to sit right beside her, like a couple, not like random strangers. He was only a hand's distance away. "As much as I like it when you call me Sir, I asked you to call me Declan."

"Okay, Declan." Yuki paused to study him. He was simply a beautiful man. Out of his starchy suits, he was even more attractive. More human, more touchable. "I'm glad you came."

"So am I. You look stunning, as always." His eyes traced her body, gaze skimming over her silver shift dress. She shivered. That intense look of his, the depth in his flashing blue eyes, had her filled with anticipation. "Great dress. You look like a movie star."

"Thanks." The dress had done its job. It was probably overkill, but she loved to dress up. And it was Christmas Eve after all. "I was in the mood to celebrate. Christmas bonus, remember. I get paid tomorrow."

He chucked, a sound that resonated low in her abdomen, tugging at muscles she'd almost forgotten she had. Then he raised his right hand and placed it over hers, on the table top. "You're my Christmas bonus, if you don't mind my being cheesy."

She didn't mind, not one cheesy bit. She loved cheese. Her luck was totally changing. His hand was large and warm on hers, and the scent of his aftershave, like the sea breeze in summer with a hint of warm spice, wrapped around her. "I've never been anyone's Christmas bonus before." She took a breath, finding him watching her, focusing on her lips.

Yuki swallowed, her mouth suddenly dry. "I meant to say, back at the hotel, I hoped your work event was okay. You looked so...down when you came back tonight."

He tipped his head to one side so a wave of his hair flopped over his forehead. "Ah, it wasn't all merry and bright. Problems with some of our investments, trusting the wrong people, that kind of thing. But I'll sort it out when I get back to Dublin."

She nodded, but something heavy sunk in the pit of her belly. "When do you fly back?"

He sighed, and suddenly he sounded exhausted. "Tomorrow night, late. Sorry, I mean tonight. I have Christmas with my Ma and Da back home. I'll just make it with the time difference."

"So soon?"

Declan threaded his fingers through hers, squeezing her hand. "I know, it's not the best timing." He caught her gaze and there was something there hiding in his eyes, a sadness that surprised her.

Yuki let go of his hand and raised hers to touch the adorable scruff on his jaw. "So? That means we have to pack a lot of fun into one day."

Then she leaned in, gently pressing her mouth to his, and tasted his lips. Delicious man. She kissed him like this was her last ever kiss, and tonight was the end of the world. Honestly, if the world was ending, she intended to go out with a bang.

Declan groaned as Yuki, this beautiful girl, pressed her mouth to his. She tasted of fruity lip gloss, mango maybe. It was officially his favourite flavour in the whole world. He leaned in to wrap his arm around her shoulders, pulling her body close to him. He licked across her lower lip and she opened for him, so he took the kiss deeper.

This time it was her turn to groan, a small sound of surrender. The sound unlocked something inside him, some vault he'd hidden away filled with pain and loneliness. He didn't feel any of that with Yuki. It was all engulfing heat. Attraction. An irresistible pull towards her.

He tilted his head, kissed the side of her mouth, then across her cheek. He wanted her, so much, but this wasn't the place. He ran his fingers through her loose hair, a silk curtain, smooth against his fingers.

"Yuki." He let his forehead rest against hers. "Where did you come from?"

"Declan. I came from Swanston Street, in an Uber." She beamed at him, her eyes sparkling with laughter.

He chuckled. "I meant, how did I happen to meet you, all the way across the world?"

"Luck."

"The luck of the Irish?"

Her lips lifted up into a sweet smile. "Something like that."

A scraping sound, a chair being dragged over concrete, had him glancing over Yuki's shoulder. A lanky blonde fellow dressed in a flannel shirt and ripped jeans had pulled his chair right up to theirs, too close for his liking.

"This is a great pub. Great vibe. Good to be back." The words brought Declan halfway back to earth. The man spoke again, watching Yuki far too closely. "Hey Yuki, who's your friend?"

She pulled away from Declan, straightening her spine. "Hi Glenn. This is Declan, visiting from Ireland. Declan,

Glenn's in my friend's band. He plays guitar."

"Aren't I your friend too?"

Yuki's posture stiffened. "Um, sure. Where's Blair?"

"She's on her way. Getting her mics and stuff out of the van."

A long-suffering sigh from Yuki told Declan exactly what she thought of this guy. "By herself? Shouldn't you help her with that?"

Glenn shrugged, apparently clueless. "Oh, yeah. Probably. I'll be right back." He loped off, heading in the direction of a side exit.

Declan asked a careful question, to gauge Yuki's reaction. "Not your favourite person?"

Yuki turned to him and whispered, "Glenn is Exhibit A in the case of me versus arseholes I used to date."

"Ah." Declan did not want to talk about Glenn The Arsehole Ex. He tried for a change of subject. "So, your friend Blair, is she a singer?"

"Oh yes, and a songwriter. She's so talented, one of those people who just lights up a room, you know?"

He touched Yuki's face, stroking the soft skin of her cheek. "Aye, I know someone like that." Declan watched the compliment sink in, Yuki's eyes sparkling in the low lighting.

This night, with this girl, it could be one of those times he'd always remember. A little festive magic was in the air. He wanted her, wanted to kiss her again. He hoped she felt the same.

An hour later, the band was on stage, they'd had a couple of drinks and Yuki was having the best time. Declan was by her side as they danced along to the music near the front of the stage. He had surprisingly good moves for an IT guy. She glanced his way and nearly lost her balance, but he grabbed her hips with his big strong hands. She nearly swooned. When he let her go, she missed his touch like her next breath.

Blair was killing it tonight. In her gold mini dress and combat boots, platinum blonde pixie haircut and with a scarlet guitar strapped to her, she was a rock goddess. Her voice was brilliant too. She belted out the Ladyhawke tune, *Magic*, the words floating over the crowd like a spell. A song about a man who lived over the Atlantic, but maybe if they were together, it could be magic. For a lifetime.

Yuki soaked in the scene. The heat and noise of the crowd faded as Declan took her hand. She reached up, her other hand on the nape of his neck. He leaned down and she kissed him, just a brief touch of lips, but enough to cause a whoosh of a flame to ignite inside her.

The band finished up the song with a string of thank yous, and Blair said, "Happy Christmas Eve, Melbourne." The crowd erupted in woops and yelling. She passed a mic to Glenn, who had been leaning slouchily near the drum kit.

He started strumming his guitar, then said, "This song's for Yuki." A gasp left her mouth in a rush, and she crossed her arms under her breasts. She recognised the start of the song, *Under The Milky Way* by The Church, one of her all time favourites. Glenn wouldn't ruin it for her. No way.

"Declan, do you mind if we get some fresh air?" She turned to find him watching her already, his eyes narrowed a little.

"No problem. This way." He ushered her through the crowd to the side of the stage, behind some massive speakers. A side door with a glowing green Exit sign marked the way out.

In less than a minute, they stumbled out of the heat and noise into fresh air, cooler than Yuki had been expecting. They were in a small courtyard dotted with a few cafe tables, strung with fairy lights overhead, stars shimmering far above in the summer sky.

The courtyard was empty and fenced off from a side street. A few smokers stood on the other side of the fence, taking in low voices. The music from inside the pub followed them, a haunting song that always gave her shivers. Goosebumps prickled her bare arms.

Declan took her hand again and pulled her towards him. "Are you okay?"

She nodded, watching for Declan's reaction. "Yeah. But Glenn has some balls dedicating a song to me. Last time I saw him, we had been hanging out at my apartment, and he told me he was going out for beer. Next thing I heard, he was in Sydney recording an album with some other band, living with some other girl. That was months ago."

His face went stony. A muscle in his jaw twitched. "He just up and left?"

"Uh huh. But I don't want to spend any more time talking about him."

Declan's expression shifted to a half smile. "In that case, will you dance with me?"

Her heart stuttered at the lines etched on his forehead, the questioning look he gave her, half expectation, half anxiety. "Yes". Of course, the answer was yes.

She stepped forward and almost fell against him, his arms wrapped around her, with her head resting against his chest. They swayed together, bodies in sync with the music. Yuki's heart picked up speed when Declan tipped her chin up with his fingertips, staring down at her with unfathomably deep blue eyes.

"Hey, you."

He kissed her, and all thoughts rushed out of her head. She was on her tiptoes, reaching for him, hands around the back of his neck, when he lifted her up and spun them around. He deepened the kiss, sliding his tongue against hers, tasting her. Her head spun with the dizzy sensation, and her little handbag fell to the ground with a thump.

One of his hands held her up, under her butt, the other roamed over her body. She moved against him, feeling his hardness pressed against her, the heat of him searing her skin through her thin dress.

He let her down, but her legs were shaky. She clung to him, and if her hand ended up under his shirt, stroking his flat stomach, so what? He kissed down her throat, his hand cupping the underside of her breast, now his thumb stroked back and forth across her hard nipple, while he licked the shell of her ear. She ached. God, she ached for him.

He took her mouth again, more possessive this time. Oh, wow. The man could kiss. How lucky could she get?

Before she knew what was happening, the song had finished and the band started playing a stupidly loud version of some Kings of Leon song. They broke apart, watching each other, both breathing heavily. His shirt was half unbuttoned where she'd tried to get at more of skin. A nice V of hair on his chest taunted her, tempted her to touch.

"Stay with me tonight?" His voice was gruff.

Yuki bit her lip. "At the hotel?" She hesitated, but only because of stupid rules. "It's not really allowed."

He shrugged, one eyebrow lifted. "Want to be a little bit naughty?"

Oh God, he was cute. She ran her hand over his jaw again, planting a fairy kiss on his mouth. "Mmmm. And a little bit nice, I hope. Let's go."

# Chapter Five

## The Palladian Hotel

### 3am on Christmas Eve

Sneaking into the hotel like a thief in the middle of the night, where he was a lawful paying guest, wasn't something Declan had on his Christmas bingo card. But with Yuki holding his hand, it was a hell of a lot of fun. Sprinting past

Reception without being seen was going to be the tricky part.

They stood behind a marble column right inside the hotel's front entrance, Yuki's body hidden from view behind him. The concierge desk was empty, closed down for the night, and the lighting in the foyer was dimmed.

Yuki swivelled this way and that, checking out the scene. She whispered, "I think we could sneak over to the elevators by the restaurant, but we'd need to be quick."

"Okay. On the count of three..."

But sleigh bells jingled from outside, someone chuckled, and a whole lot of footsteps echoed down the empty street. Someone was singing *Santa Claus is Coming To Town*.

Declan took a deep breath, then tugged on Yuki's arm. "Wait. Listen."

They both turned and stared out the large plate glass windows facing the street. Santas were coming. A whole group of them, walking, stumbling to the hotel's entrance. They had to be drunk. The singing was awful.

One of the Santas swiped a key card and the front doors swooshed open. And in they danced, all dressed up in full red and white regalia. Declan whipped his head around. He blinked at Yuki, whose mouth was hanging open. What could only be described as a conga line of Santas came dancing right past them, into the foyer.

He and Yuki glanced at each other again. He nudged her arm, then nodded in the direction of the elevator. He held up his hand, waiting for the oblivious Santas to dance past their position, singing *Frosty The Snowman* now. He nodded again, then mouthed: *three, two, one*. He went first.

They ran, along one wall, like their pants were on fire. Maybe they were, so to speak, because he'd never wanted anything more than to get Yuki into his bed. Behind him, Yuki let out a yelping noise, and he turned to find her rubbing her head, and a hatless Santa rubbing his.

"He slammed right into me," she stage-whispered in Declan's direction.

Santa was unsteady on his feet. He pointed at Yuki. "Sorry. Wait... You're the nice one from Reception. The one who found me the good whiskey." The man's head turned as if in slow-motion to Declan, giving him the once over. "You sneaking in?"

Declan nodded, craning his neck to see if the night manager had heard all the noise. Ten metres of foyer separated them from

Reception, and no one was walking their way. They were safe, for now.

Yuki said, "He's my boyfriend. I'm not supposed to stay here overnight."

Declan's face heated and his grin was probably manic. *Boyfriend?* He liked the sound of that.

The hatless Santa frowned, his stick-on beard flapping on one side. "Bah humbug! Leave it to me." He tapped the side of his nose with one finger.

He dashed over to one of his younger man-in-red-suit friends, grabbed him by the collar and dragged him over. "Give the girl your hat and jacket." The other man shrugged, his eyes unfocused, and mildly confused.

"Yuki. That's my name." Yuki took the offered costume and quickly put it on over her dress. She swam in it, petite as she was. She tucked her hair into her jacket and adjusted her hat, then caught Declan's eyes. Her dark eyes sparkled with mischief. She was cute as a button, or a fake Mrs Claus on the run from the law.

The first man nodded, saying under his breath, "I'm Brian, but you can call me Kris Kringle." Brian/Kris grabbed his own jacket by the lapels and took it off, handing it to Declan. Declan dressed too, scanning the space for the manager at the same time.

Declan thought he knew the plan now. Pretend to be Santas, blend in. It was just ridiculous enough that it might work, at least at three o'clock in the morning on Christmas Eve.

Brian moved with relative grace for a man who had a naturally Santa-esque frame, moving to push Declan and Yuki into line in front of him. They soon caught up to the rest of the staggering Santas, halfway across the foyer, now singing a rousing rendition of *Rudolph The Red Nosed Reindeer*.

They simply joined in singing, formed a conga line and headed across the large open plan space. Yuki ducked behind Declan, half giggling, half humming. When they were near the elevator, Brian turned and gave Declan the thumbs up.

Declan dashed to the right, holding Yuki's hand, pulling her with him round the corner to the elevator in a cul-de-sac. He slammed his hand onto the Up button. In the distance, he heard Brian give a hearty "Ho, ho, ho!", no doubt distracting the manager on the Reception desk.

Declan and Yuki looked into each other's eyes and broke into silent laughter. The elevator car came, and they hopped aboard. No kissing, no touching, Declan was a good boy and kept a polite distance from Yuki at all times. But the

tension between them was an invisible
force, keeping their eyes on each other.
Connected.

Yuki waited, hopping from foot to foot in
her heels, as Declan scanned his key card
on the electronic lock on the door to the
Executive Suite on the twenty fifth floor.
The door clicked open, and then they were
inside.

The suite's lights clicked on now, only a
hazy golden glow from the lamp by the bed
and a crack of light from the bathroom. It
was a gorgeous room, probably as big as
her whole apartment. Silver grey walls and
black and white silk bedding said luxury,
in a rich-people understated way. But there
was a modern crystal chandelier, sparkling

in the low light, which set the whole thing off in her humble opinion.

She didn't want to waste any more time. Declan was just ahead of her, tossing his wallet and keys on the wooden side table. He still wearing his Santa jacket. She tugged on his fur-trimmed sleeve, so he turned to face her. Then he grabbed his jacket by the lapels and pulled him closer. She ran her hands over his biceps, stroking him. Then she was trying to get the jacket off, fiddling with Velcro tabs.

Declan huffed out a breath on a half laugh. "Woah, what's the rush?"

Yuki blinked at him. "Are you freaking kidding me? Kiss me already, you great Irish fool."

He grabbed her waist as he chuckled, deep and throaty. "As you wish."

He pressed his lips down upon hers, like she was the rain and he was a parched man in the desert. She squeaked out of the corner of her mouth as he licked across her lower lip, then bit it, gently. Yuki kissed him back, melting into him, closing her eyes against the rush of heat, the ache taking over her body.

She didn't want to rely on her legs to hold her upright, so she jumped on him. It was only logical. He caught her, wrapped her legs around his back and held her there, grinding against her in such a way...she knew he wanted her. And she needed him. Now.

Yuki groaned, breaking their kiss. "Oh my gawwwwd...quick! Take your clothes off."

"Alright, alright." He laughed again, and she felt the reverberation of it under her hands.

She was unbuttoning his shirt, with fumbling, shaking hands. And they were moving. Declan had spun them around and was walking them towards the bed. A second later he let her go and plopped her down on the bed like a sack of potatoes.

"Hey!"

But then she raised her eyes and saw what he was doing. He yanked off his red jacket and pulled his shirt straight over his head, muscles in his stomach and chest tensing and flexing with the action. His hair stood up, waves all gorgeous and messy. He was beautiful. Not thin, built with slabs of corded muscles, dusted in dark hair. A small black tattoo, a Celtic design on his bicep, had her salivating. She wanted to taste his skin, all over. His eyes were wild as he stared down at her.

She ripped off her Santa hat and shook out her hair, then got rid of her own red jacket, tossing it on the floor. Yuki kept her eyes on Declan, as her pulse thudded in her ears, and between her legs. With a quick move, her silver sheath dress was unzipped and she shimmied it down and off. It slithered off her legs, leaving her in nothing but her black silky bra and underwear.

"Oh, Miss Yuki. Look at you. So gorgeous." He popped open the button on his jeans, and she bit her lip. He toed off his sneakers, kicked them away, then tugged down his jeans. She breathed out at the sight of him, wearing only in black boxers.

He came to her, climbing onto the edge of the bed beside her. The first thing he did, literally first, was lean down and kiss her belly button. A flick of his tongue there had her gasping. He ran one big hand down over her underwear, stroking her.

He looked up at her, his eyes in shadow. He pulled aside the fabric and touched her, making her squirm. "Do you want me to kiss you here?"

She leaned back on her elbows, watching him. "Yes, but later. Come here."

He crawled up her body until he lay partly on top of her, still it was an awkward shuffle until he was pressed fully against her. She kissed his chest, the base of his throat, nuzzling there until he groaned and slid the strap of her bra down one shoulder.

Declan pulled down the silk fabric so her breast was exposed, and then his mouth was on her flesh, kissing and sucking her sensitive nipple. In two seconds flat, she had wriggled her bra off and he was kissing her other breast, cupping it with his big hand, teasing her. She was so on edge already, she was panting, the feeling was so intense.

Pressing his lips to her throat, he murmured, "Yuki, I want you."

She nodded, catching her breath. "Me too. Do you have protection?"

He placed a sweet kiss on her cheek. "Wait here, don't move." He climbed off her, dashed over to the table where he'd left his wallet and then he was back again.

Back on the bed, he sat beside her, and she propped herself on her side, watching him. His boxers came off, then the hard length of him sprang up, straining almost against his flat stomach. She swallowed, hard, as he tore open the condom wrapper in his hand, and rolled it over himself in a fluid motion.

When he looked up at her, she simply reached out for him, and then they were together. He peeled off her knickers, and he touched her again, exactly where she was aching. They tangled in a mass of arms and legs, mostly hers, wrapped high around his waist.

He placed kisses down her neck, to her lips, his hands roaming on her body. He slid a hand between them and stroked her, until Yuki was ready and rocking beneath him, trying to get closer. Close as possible.

"Declan, please," she said. She wasn't too proud to beg, especially when it got results.

He gripped her hip and rocked into her, until he slid right inside her. So good. So perfect. Yuki let a full lungful of air gush out of her lips, before biting Declan's shoulder and kissing him. Kissing him. Always kissing him.

Their hips worked, and Yuki surged up to meet Declan, over and over, until she shook with need. He raised himself up on his strong forearms and thrust into her, once, twice, taking her over the edge with him as they floated on a cloud, silver stars falling in the night sky behind her eyelids.

Later, she snuggled in the huge bed next to Declan, who totally hogged the covers. She blinked and opened her eyes, rubbed up against the roughness of his leg hair, and flung her own leg over his.

Declan rolled over and kissed her lips. "Hey, Miss Yuki. I think I'm falling for this girl. Do you think I should tell her? Yes or no?"

Her heart flipped over, doing somersaults. "Yes. Always yes. And you should kiss her. A lot."

His twisted half smile, like he was trying to be serious, was totally adorable. "Noted." He cleared his throat, then said in a dramatic deep voice, "Yuki, I think I'm falling for you."

Yuki let the warm glow spreading through her body show itself on her face, her cheek muscles stretching out with the force of her grin. She snuggled closer to Declan until she could kiss him, tugging his lower lip with her teeth. He made a noise like, "Hmmmpf" and flipped her onto her back.

Then he was moving down the bed, kissing her belly button again. "A lot of kisses, huh?" He raised his eyebrows before he flipped the sheet over his head and kissed a path all the way down, to exactly where she wanted him.

"Oh, Declan!"

# Chapter Six

## The Palladian Hotel

**Late morning, Christmas Eve**

Declan was usually up with the birds, whether he liked it or not. Not this morning though. He'd slept like a bear hibernating for the winter. Only his phone woke him up, rousing the drowsy and cranky bear. Whoever it was, making him get out of bed while Yuki was still in it, warm and soft, cuddling up to him, better be warned. He was in a mood. It stopped ringing.

He grabbed his phone off the bedside table, rolling out of bed and crossing the room in his boxers to stand near the windows. Three missed calls, all from Kendra. Oh hell. It rang again in his hand. "Ah, shit."

He took the call, trying not to completely lose his cool. "Declan."

"Well, hello. I've been trying to call for ages. What on earth are you doing?"

Declan sighed, grabbing a clean t-shirt from his suitcase and dragging it over his head. "Sleeping, or I was. What's the problem, Kendra?"

She paused, and he steeled himself for whatever bad news she was about to fling at him. "I didn't want to do this over the phone, but I couldn't find you yesterday.

I wanted to tell you personally that I'm handing in my resignation."

Declan waited for a stone of cold anger to hit, as per usual when he talked to his ex, but it was strangely absent. "Okay. Do you want to talk severance packages? Jon will be in touch once I have it in writing."

He could almost hear her choking on the other end of the phone. "That's it? You don't want to talk me out of it?"

He sat heavily in the armchair by the windows, opening the curtains a crack. It was blindingly bright out. "Not really. I did the best for you that I could, after our breakup. But you had to make a dog's breakfast of the job here in Melbourne. That was not only cruel, it was unprofessional too. And I think you know it. I'll be cleaning up after you for months. Tell me when you want to finish up."

"Effective immediately. I have another job starting in the new year."

Declan shrugged. "Fine. Email me your letter of resignation and Jon will sort out the details."

"But Declan, don't you want to know where I'm going?" The whine in her voice was grating on his nerves.

"Not really, no." He ended the call. Maybe it was juvenile to cut her off like that, but he was so done with her.

He stared at his phone for a second, then spotted the actual time. Eleven fifteen. He turned to the bed, to see the gorgeous girl with her jet black hair fanned put on the pillow, her delicate curves covered only by a sheet.

He was pretty sure Yuki didn't have to work today, but she was sound asleep in the Executive Suite, upstairs from the very same people she had been trying to dodge last night. She probably wouldn't be happy about still being here with him.

Declan thought about climbing back into bed, but he wouldn't get back to sleep. Not now. So he headed for the shower. He needed the hot water, his back was a bit sore (for good reasons) and most of all, he needed time to think, before he talked to Yuki.

He didn't want to end things with her. But would a long-distance relationship be something she was open to? Declan wasn't superstitious, but her crossed his fingers and made a Christmas wish. Hopefully, Yuki would still be his, after they had a chance to talk.

Yuki pretended to be asleep long enough to hear most of the conversation Declan had with his ex. So, she was resigning, saying goodbye. It didn't sound too warm and fuzzy. Good. Yuki wanted Declan all to herself, no use denying it.

She rolled over when Declan closed the bathroom door, and then she heard the shower running. With a glance at the clock on her side of the bed, she sat bolt upright. After eleven? Nearly lunchtime?

"Oh no! No, no, no..."

Yuki jumped out of bed and scampered to find her clothes. Just her little silver dress and a Santa jacket? "No!" She couldn't go downstairs looking like that.

She groaned with frustration as she put on her underwear and dress, baulking at the Santa gear. Imagine if she waltzed past her co-workers dressed like that. They would think she was delusional. If the shift manager saw her, she'd be out on her ear.

*Melanie*. She could help Yuki out of this mess. Maybe?

Yuki crossed the room to where her handbag lay on the table next to Declan's wallet. Fishing out her phone, she went to text Mel. She already had a message:

**Melanie:** *Don't come downstairs. Security video! BTW nice hat Mrs Claus. Declan looks sexy ;)*

"Noooo!"

The shower was still running in the bathroom. She flicked her head in that direction. Should she stay and talk to Declan, ask him to help her come up with a solution? He was a good man, but he'd have no idea how to help. No. She had to handle this, somehow.

She wrote a quick note on the hotel's fancy stationery, added her phone number, and searched in the wardrobe for one Declan's business shirts.

Yuki quickly popped on a white shirt over her dress, tied a knot in the front to bring it to mid-thigh length, almost completely covering her shiny dress. She tied her hair in a low ponytail and donned her sunglasses too. She checked her reflection in the mirror on the wardrobe door. With her head down, she was almost incognito. She could be any old guest walking out the front door. Hopefully.

"Right. Let's do this."

She was about to make a dash for it, when the bathroom door opened. A cloud of steam and a damp Declan, dressed only in a towel slung low on his hips, emerged with a sexy swagger in his walk. His trademark grin faded as he checked out her outfit, complete with shoes and sunglasses.

His eyebrows lifted, his brow creased. "Going somewhere?"

Her heart stalled for a moment. She had to explain. She yanked off her sunnies. "Oh Declan. It's the worst! Melanie texted me and said I shouldn't go downstairs and there's security video of me in a Santa hat from last night. I'm soooo fired!"

He grimaced, then moved towards her. "Were you just going to leave, without a word?"

"No. I mean yes, but I wrote you a note." She pointed at the table.

Silently, he walked to the table and grabbed the note, reading it in a few seconds. It was brief, it was true. He read it out loud:

*Dear Declan,*

*Had a fun night! Hope to see you later. Call me if you want.*

*Yuki.*

"You added a smiley face. At least you gave me your number before bailing on me. That's something, I guess." His voice was cold as a shard of ice.

Yuki shook her head. "It's not like that. I loved our night together. Honest. I just need to find a way out of here. That's all I can think about for now."

Declan shrugged. "I guess you're going then. I was going to suggest we have breakfast in bed, but if that's not what you want—"

Yuki's face heated. She did want to stay. But he was making this situation all about him! Couldn't he see she was trapped? "I do want to stay, really, but I can't forget about my job, my life, just to hang out with you for a bit longer! You're the one leaving the country tonight."

He stared at her, boring down into the depths of her soul, or it felt like it. "I thought we had something good going on. There could be more than one night. But

I guess I was wrong. Wouldn't be the first time." He turned his back on her, and walked slowly back into the bathroom, shutting the door behind him with a definite bang.

She spoke quietly in the empty room. "Oh, hell in a handbag. What have I done?"

Yuki grabbed her things, slunk out of the suite and headed straight down the corridor for the elevator they'd taken last night. If she emerged near the restaurant downstairs, she could cut through the dining room and exit onto the side street, totally bypassing Reception. That was the plan.

By the time she hopped out on the Ground floor, she knew she'd made an obvious mistake. Security cameras. The assistant manager, Mr Ivanov, was waiting for her. Yuki's heart pounded, and it was lucky she was wearing sunglasses because her eyes were watery too. Mr Ivanov wasn't a bad guy, he was generally fair, but he looked extremely disappointed. It cut her deeper than she expected.

His dark brown eyes narrowed, exaggerating the crow's feet pattern of lines on his tanned face. Mr Ivanov squinted at her appearance. "Ms Yamimoto. Would you please accompany me to my office?"

She simply nodded and followed him, dragging her feet as if she was a condemned prisoner walking to her own execution. On the way past Reception, she blinked as Carlos shot her a sympathetic smile, and mouthed the words, *Call me.*

Declan didn't really expect her to be there when he'd got himself under control, brushed off the stupid dampness on his

cheeks, and came out of the bathroom.
He'd hoped she'd be there, maybe waiting
for him back in bed. But that was fantasy
stuff, not real life. Real life was being left,
again, by a girl he liked a lot more than
was sensible. He huffed out a deep breath
and sat down on the edge of the bed in the
silent room.

Yuki was a dream girl, not part of his
everyday grind. He'd pack his suitcase, get
ready to fly home, spend Christmas with
his family, get back to work and forget all
about her.

Except he wouldn't forget about her,
because he knew he was lying to himself.
He clenched his fists, then got up, got
dressed, dragging on his jeans and a
business shirt. He had to make a couple
of calls. The world didn't stop because his
heart was beaten up and bruised purple,
again.

Declan had to speak to Jon about the whole Kendra thing. He had to decide on the best course of action, and suddenly one option appeared in his mind like the proverbial pot of gold at the end of the rainbow. Maybe he was a sucker, chasing something that didn't exist. But he had to try to fix things, both the business-related mess in the Melbourne office and the personal mess with Yuki.

He made the call. He'd take a chance. He crossed his fingers for luck.

Yuki didn't usually cry at work, but today was a special occasion. She had never been fired before. She'd nodded along with Mr Ivanov's account of what happened the night before. Yes, she had dated a hotel guest. Yes, that was her entering the hotel at three o'clock in the morning, wearing a Santa hat. Yes, she had spent the night with a guest in his hotel suite.

She didn't want to say anymore, but one phrase slipped out, "I really like him. I didn't want to cause any trouble, but I just really...like him." It sounded pathetic, but it was true.

Mr Ivanov nodded, sighed in an exhausted way, and patted her on the hand. He passed her a box of Kleenex before he left his office, to organise her termination papers and final pay cheque. No Christmas bonus, of course.

Yuki blew her nose into a tissue, and then grabbed her phone from her bag. She messaged Melanie.

**Yuki:** *I'M FIRED. I knew it, but it still sucks. I hope we can still be friends.*

Melanie replied immediately.

*Melanie: Yes it sucks! Of course we're still friends you big dork! Come see me before you leave, if you can. x*

At least she still had one friend among her co-workers. The image of Carlos popped into her head. She texted him too.

*Yuki: I'm fired. Happy to hang out sometime though if you still want to keep in touch.*

*Carlos: Yes! Come to dinner with me and Zack in the new year.*

Yuki smiled, and blew her nose again. Carlos and his boyfriend Zack were both lovely guys. And Zack was a chef, so his choice of dinner was bound to be awesome.

*Carlos: But first...do you want to leave a note at Reception for your favourite guest?*

Yuki froze, staring at her phone. She could do that, send a goodbye note to Declan. No one except Carlos would need to know. But she didn't think she could stroll up to Reception on her way out of the hotel. No, she would leave a note with Melanie and ask her to pass it on.

**Yuki:** *Thanks, you're a gem. I'll be in touch.*

She smiled, then sucked in a breath, slapping a hand over her mouth. She had an idea. If the universe truly hated her, it wouldn't work. But if there was a glimmer of hope, a thing called fate or whatever, she had to try.

The thing she had with Declan could be special, she knew it in her bones. So, she planned out what she would write, everything she'd do, to make sure he knew exactly how she felt. Before he left for Ireland.

Her phone pinged again with another message. No, it was an email. The email she had been waiting for, finally. With trembling fingers, she opened it and read it super quick, then read over it again, making sure of the details.

She squealed so loud she was certain Mr Ivanov would think she'd completely lost her mind. Maybe she had, but in a good way. Only time would tell...

# Chapter Seven

## The Palladian Hotel

**2pm on Christmas Eve**

Declan headed to Reception to check out, and to order a taxi headed to the airport. Sure, he would be a few hours early for his flight, but he could hang out in the Business Class lounge and get some work done. He wanted nothing more than to get the hell out of the hotel, ASAP.

He wheeled his suitcase behind him as he approached the Reception desk, looking about from side to side, warily. Hopefully the hotel manager wasn't about to accost him and yell at him for corrupting one of his staff.

Declan wouldn't have entirely blamed him. Yuki was younger than him, and she'd been at work when they met. She had warned him when they headed back to the hotel, said it wasn't allowed, but did that stop Declan? Nope. He'd been under the influence of lust, pure and simple. It wasn't like him, at all. Usually, he was in complete control. Cold as a robot, according to Kendra.

When he stood in front of the desk, he half expected Yuki to pop out of the back office and banter with him. But it was a young man, Carlos, her friend maybe, who asked if he could help with anything.

"Wait just one moment, sir." He made a quick phone call, and Declan waited. "Our Events Manager will be down in a moment. She has a matter to discuss with you, if you'd be kind enough to wait."

Declan stared blankly at Carlos. What was this about? Then he remembered: the mezzanine, a snow machine, Yuki spinning around in the pretty white flakes, Santa on a throne being yelled at by her friend with curly hair... Melanie, the Events Manager.

"Yes, sure." Declan stepped to one side, wheeling his suitcase to a spot against a wall, in front of a mini Christmas tree. Carlos nodded, then shot him a wide smile.

Melanie arrived on the scene, her curls bouncing as she speed-walked towards him. "Mr Moriarty, it's a pleasure to meet you." She extended her right hand and he shook it, not sure what was happening. Melanie grinned, placing a large envelope in his other hand.

"I do hope you'll read this over this proposal, Mr Moriarty. The Events Team and many of the staff will be sorry to see you leave before we have had a chance to discuss certain future events. I'm sure you, um, your company, will keep us in mind. For the future."

Very cryptic. He nodded, and Melanie took his hand again. "Good. I'll be around until seven tonight, if you need anything. Anything at all." She turned and walked away.

He stared after her, then glanced at the envelope in his hand, marked only with his name. Opening it, he laughed as a pile of gold glitter tumbled out. He had a feeling now, this letter could only be from Yuki.

He unfolded the paper, read it, careful not to get too much glitter on his shirt.

*To Declan,*

*I'm so sorry I'm not telling you this in person, but I couldn't let you leave the country without telling you how I feel. I'm mad about you. That's basically it. But I want to tell you the whole story.*

*From the first second I saw you, looking all handsome, I thought I'd love to go out with you. Well, to be honest I thought I'd like to kiss the big white smile right off your face. Then you spoke to me (I was sitting under the Christmas tree, do you remember?) and you had an Irish accent and Oh My God, I nearly swallowed my tongue. I adore an Irish accent, did you know that? You were my idea of perfect. But I never thought you'd really like me.*

*Anyway, we haven't had nearly enough time to get to know each other, but I wanted* to tell you that last night was the BEST night of my life, even if I did get fired. It was totally worth it! Even now, thinking about how you touched me...my face is on fire. Other parts of me too. The fun parts, if you know what I mean?

I want you to know, I like you, a lot. So much, I feel like my heart is going to explode, like a letter full of glitter. Is that a weird thing to say? I don't care. I think I've fallen in love with you, even though I've only known you a few days and that's probably ridiculous. Sometimes I jump into things head first without thinking things through...you might have noticed!

Please don't leave without saying goodbye, properly. If I haven't burnt my bridges or traumatised you with glitter, I'd like to invite you to my apartment to talk. We can have dinner if you want to. I want you to come over. Just in case I wasn't clear, again.

*My address in Elwood is below.*
*Lots of love (and kisses),*
*Yuki xxx*
*P.S. When you were dressed up as Santa*
*and you kissed me, that was totally a*
*fantasy of mine. That was probably a weird*
*thing to tell you too. But I'm glad I did.*

Declan folded the letter and chuckled under his breath. Yuki was some girl. She could still be *his* girl, if he played his cards right.

He wandered back to the Reception desk in a haze of conflicting emotions. He wanted her, yes. But he had to make her understand, he was a busy man. His life wasn't all neatly wrapped up in a box marked 'boyfriend material'. He wouldn't be around all the time. She might not want him if she understood all that. But then again, she might.

He glanced up to find Carlos watching him, his eyes sparkling. Declan stuffed the letter in his back pocket.

"Do you want me to order you a taxi to the airport, sir? Or somewhere else if you prefer?" Carlos was obviously a friend of Yuki's too. Good to know.

Declan smiled, he couldn't help it. "Elwood, thanks. I have to see a friend before I fly out."

The joy on Carlos's face was clear as day. "Excellent, sir."

## Yuki's apartment

## Elwood, Melbourne

Yuki dashed around her apartment like a busy bee in springtime, tidying up already tidy tables and her spotless little kitchen. She was dressed in her pink underwear and a giant Hard Candy band shirt, with a picture of a shattered candy cane. Perfect for Christmas.

Her flatmate Claudia was already gone for Christmas break, having headed to the country to stay with her family. So, she had the place all to herself, luckily. Declan might be coming over, hopefully, if he'd read her letter. If he still liked her. If her wish came true. She wanted everything to be ready.

She danced along to the radio, into her bedroom. She straightened the silver quilt on her bed, fluffed the pillows and lit a few vanilla scented candles on the side tables. There. Everything was pretty and ready. Her stomach rolled over. She wasn't ready!

She sprinted to her wardrobe and scanned her options. Little red dress? Super festive, but maybe too much with all the sequins? Blue spaghetti strap sundress? Cute-sexy. That was a winner. She was about to get changed when the apartment's door buzzer went off.

She checked her reflection in the bedroom mirror. "Um, you'll have to do. You're super cute, Yuki. Any man would be lucky to have you." She breathed out slowly. She didn't quite believe the affirmations that Melanie suggested she practice, but maybe they helped her confidence, a little.

She made her way to the front door, answering the intercom. "Who is it?"

"Declan." His voice was extra deep. Sexy. She bit her lip.

"Please, come upstairs." She danced on the spot while she waited, trying to get rid of her nerves. He knocked a few moments later, and she unlocked the door, flinging it wide open.

He was beautiful. A lock of hair flopped over his forehead, and his blue shirt matched the shade of his eyes. The force of him struck her again, like some kind of mystical lightning. He leaned on his suitcase, and she wished he was staying with her.

"Declan." Yuki grinned, her heart hammering as she stepped back to let him inside. "Thank you so much for coming over. My flatmate is a guerrilla knitter, be warned. She's gone away for a few days." She extended her arm to show him in and closed the door behind him.

He was close enough to smell the scent of his aftershave. She wanted to kiss his gorgeous face. Take him straight to the bedroom. But he brushed past her, without meeting her eyes. She didn't want it to go this way, all cold and formal.

Now Declan tipped his head to one side, and she felt his eyes on her, running up and down the length of her body. His face was serious though. "Should I ask what on earth a guerrilla knitter is?"

"Come through to the lounge room, you'll see."

Declan left his suitcase near the front door, glanced around the apartment and he soon figured out the guerrilla knitter thing. Lamps were wrapped in multi-coloured knitted cosies, knitted wall hangings decorated every spare inch of space, even a knitted plant holder sat on the coffee table, a wilting fern almost hidden inside it. A small silver Christmas tree sat on the kitchen counter, covered in knitted decorations. Guerrilla knitting, indeed.

Yuki ushered him over to a big blue sofa, and he followed her, watching as the fabric of the t-shirt she wore swayed when she walked. It barely covered her round little bottom. He swallowed, hard.

He sat on one end of the sofa, and he thought she'd stick to the other end. But she sat only a couple of inches away. Her bare thighs taunted him, daring him to touch.

He cleared his throat. "I got your letter." He held up his palm, so she could see the sparkles clinging to his skin. He was ridiculously nervous, and his hand shook.

She laughed, and pressed her hand to his, threaded their fingers together. He let out a long breath.

"Yuki, I—"

"Declan, I meant—"

He laughed, and she did too. The ice was broken. "You go first," he said, watching her face go soft, a gentle expression of...love? Caring, at least.

She let her words come out in a great rush. "I meant to tell you how much I already care about you. But then, I thought I was going to lose my job, and I panicked. It was all too much, all at once. I really wanted to spend more time with you."

Declan lifted her hand to his mouth and kissed the back of her hand, and something inside him relaxed when he heard her sigh. "Did you actually lose your job? Because I'd feel terrible about that."

She let a quasi-smile cross her face, one dimple creasing her cheek. "Yes. But it's okay now. I didn't get a chance to tell you, I interviewed for another job a few weeks ago. Actually, it was three interviews, and I thought I must be on the shortlist. I got it! I just found out this afternoon."

He watched her eyes, lit up with excitement. "That's grand. Tell me about it." He half listened to her answer, all the while watching her lips.

"I'm going to be a flight attendant with Mermaid Airlines! You know, the funnest airline in the world. It's so exciting because I've always wanted to travel, but I haven't been anywhere except here, and Japan and Singapore with my family when I was a kid. So anyway, I have to fly out in a few days for training, in London!"

"London? But I thought...I thought you'd be living here." He held his breath, waiting for what she'd say next.

Yuki pushed her loose hair back behind her ear. "It's only for a couple of weeks. They want me back in Melbourne as my home base, as well as flying to lots of cool places. But I'd love to move to London one day."

Declan's heart had swelled in his chest, but it relaxed again until he could breathe properly. "That's grand. I mean, fantastic. I organised some work stuff too, rearranged things so I could be here for a few months. In Melbourne."

Her mouth popped open, and he wanted to kiss her, right that second. "You did? Why, Declan?"

No use beating around the bush now. "Partly for work-related reasons. Someone who knows the business needs to take the reins in the Asia Pacific office, so it might as well be me. But mostly, for you, Miss Yuki. I wanted to stay here, to see more of you. To take you out, to stay in with you. To kiss you. A lot."

Her smile grew from something fragile, to a full bloom across her pretty face. "Oh.

In that case..." She shuffled across until she sat on his lap. "Merry Christmas to me."

"Merry Christmas to me, too."

Then he kissed her delicious lips. He kept right on kissing her until they were both short of breath. God, he couldn't get enough of her. The way she was squirming on his lap told him she felt the same way. He palmed her firm bottom, squeezing her flesh through the soft shirt she wore like a dress. Heat and the promise of pleasure thundered through his whole body.

Yuki pulled away from their kiss and touched his cheek. "Come with me."

Yuki took Declan's hand, the one still covered in glitter, and led him straight to her bedroom. He was mostly quiet, but when he entered the room fully, he whispered, "I've been dying to see your bedroom."

"Really? It's not that fancy."

Declan looked around the room and said, "It's totally you. Those little stars on the ceiling, the silver curtains, the pink armchair, the quotes and postcards on the wall. All of it." He faced her again, pulling her into a hug, close to his body. She rested her head on his broad chest. "Sweet, pretty, full of fun and dreams."

She shrugged, but heat flooded her face. "Huh. You like it, then?"

He spoke low in her ear. "I love it. Adore it, really." He kissed the base of her throat.

*Oh, hello heart explosion!* She didn't have it in her to play it cool, when he was being so adorable himself. She lifted her head, meeting his eyes. "Get in my bed. What are you waiting for?"

He laughed, low and rumbly. "Such a polite invitation."

Okay, maybe she did need to cool it, a bit. But he moved towards the bed and started removing his clothes, so that was the important thing. First his shirt went, tossed on her pink chair, revealing acres of lovely man-skin.

Then he unbuttoned the fly of his jeans and she had to press a hand to her mouth. He was...bigger, in the daylight. Of course she remembered the feel of him, the pressure inside her when they came together, everything just right. Now everything low in her abdomen tightened, in memory, in anticipation.

His shoes and the jeans were gone in a moment, and his grey boxer briefs were stupidly sexy, in that unassuming guy way. He probably didn't even know he had that poet-slash-rockstar thing going on, the way he flexed his bicep with his interesting tattoo. He looked at her from under a lock of his thick wavy hair.

Yuki let out a long, shaky breath. She still had far too many clothes on. So, she jumped up on her bed, dragged her shirt up over her head and tossed it away. She shook out her hair, hoping she looked nicely rumpled and not like a hot mess. When she raised her eyes again, Declan was standing there like a statue, still halfway across the room. His eyes were on her, the smoulder of his stare burning her up from the inside out.

"God, Yuki. Look at you." He stalked over to the bed, climbing up to meet her, pushing her down gently so she rested on her pillows. "So beautiful."

Declan must have liked her hot pink lace underwear. His hands were all over her knickers, and then, *oh yes*, inside them. He kissed her lips, slowly, pressing kisses to the corners of her mouth, then down her throat again, making her want...more. She gasped when he made his way down to her breasts, kissing her right through the fabric of her skimpy bra.

"Declan," she breathed, "I want you now. I want to ride you."

"Grrrrmph." He bit down on her nipple, making her full-on squeal. He rolled off her, eyes wide, lips wet from kissing, looking completely wild. "Condom?"

"I bought a whole lot of them. See?" She pulled open the drawer of her bedside table. Piles of colourful condoms spilled out.

Declan raised an arched eyebrow. "Now I'm going to have performance anxiety."

She bit her lip. "Oh, no pressure, I only wanted to be prepared. And I liked the colours."

He grinned, showing lots of teeth. "Joking! I was messing with you." Grabbing a condom, a nice royal blue, he sat on the edge of the bed and got rid of his underwear. He prepared to sheath himself, but Yuki wanted to touch him.

"Let me." She shuffled over to him, to sit on her knees beside him. "God, you're built. I mean, I love your body, Declan."

He groaned, handing over the condom. She took her time, running her hand over the hard length of him, circling him, squeezing just a little...

"Yuki, please." His voice cracked on her name. Oooh, she liked that. Who was begging now?

In a second she sheathed him, and then she peeled off her remaining scraps of clothes. Totally naked, she straddled him, wrapping her legs around his strong back.

His eyes were on her, on every inch of her. She shivered.

When she first raised herself up, then sank down on him, he filled her so completely, she could hardly breathe. Declan's face was pressed to her neck, and the sound he made nearly brought on her climax. So gruff, so deep.

She shifted, rising and falling, rocking her hips. Yuki pressed herself down, hard, and found her rhythm. Declan rose beneath her too, giving her what she needed, angling his hips. He kissed her deeply, tasting her, pressing his body to hers, until she was undone. Her heart throbbed as the heat inside her unfurled, spread, took her over. She threw back her head, cried out, and chased the stars.

Declan held her, a firm hand on her waist. Grinding himself against her, thrusting again and again. He called her

name when he fell back, limp and spent.
And she lay on top of him, smoothing her
hand over his chest, caressing him, so glad
to have found him. So happy to love him.

"Yuki? Are you awake?" Declan whispered
the words by Yuki's cheek. She was lying
beside him, her head on her pillow, eyes
closed, beautiful as an angel.

"Mmmm. Maybe."

He chuckled, stroking her cheek with his
thumb. "Hey Miss Yuki, I'll have to leave
soon."

She sat up suddenly, the sheets dropping
away from her perfect breasts. "What? Not
already?" She brushed a strand of her hair
out of her face.

He couldn't help stroking her hair,
then stroking her breast. "It's nearly nine

o'clock. My flight's at quarter to midnight, but I'll have to get a move on."

She dropped back down to lie next to him, and kissed him, and his heart could hardly take it. He didn't want to go. He'd never wanted to stay with someone more, than with her, at that moment.

"Stay, a bit longer. Have some dessert."

They had already had dinner, in bed, home delivery from some restaurant where she knew the chef. "I think I had my dessert, even seconds. You were delicious."

"Mmmm."

He sighed, placing his hand on her waist. "What are you doing for Christmas? You haven't told me."

She glanced up at him, her eyes dancing. "I'm having lunch with my parents, and my brother's back home from Singapore. Maybe my aunts and cousins will be there. We'll eat a turkey, and sushi, and Pavlova, then play a ruthless game of Monopoly. It should be fun."

Declan squeezed her waist, let his hand wander lower to her hip. "It sounds like fun. I wish I was staying."

Yuki pressed a kiss on his cheek. "You know, I think you're the first man I'd like to bring home, to meet my family."

His chest felt too tight. She was so sweet. He felt the same, knew his parents would absolutely love her. "Not Glenn the Arsehole Ex?"

She rolled her eyes. "Urgh. He said he thought it was cool I'm Japanese, well, my family is. He wanted to collect girlfriends from the world. As if we were commemorative plates and he needed the complete set."

He sat up, crossing his arms. "Right, do you need me to hunt him down?"

She shook her head. "No, I want you to come back and see me soon, not have to find bail money."

He nodded. "Fair point." He kissed her forehead, then her lips. "I will be back soon, you know. We can do this, have dessert, whatever you want."

Yuki smiled, her cheeks rosy and warm when he touched her there. "Oh, you'd better be back soon. I can hardly wait."

She leaned over and grabbed another little coloured packet from the bedside table. "Here, you'd better give me something else to dream about." She waved the packet in his face, as he flipped her over and growled in her ear.

"Yes, Miss Yuki. Anything you want."

# Chapter Eight

## Mermaid Airlines
## Head Office,
## London, UK

**Two weeks later...**

Yuki did her best to shimmy in time
to the music along with the other
airline recruits, but her belly was full
of ninja-fighting butterflies and she felt

like an uncoordinated loser. Who knew you had to learn a weirdo dance to be a Mermaid Airlines flight attendant? Apparently, everyone else who went for the job already knew. And they could dance.

Falling off her high heels as she did a twist to her right, Yuki slammed right into the pretty blonde girl in full uniform, standing behind her. She'd got her right in the stomach. "Ooof, I'm so sorry!"

The Trainer at the front of the room shook her head, then threw her hands in the air. "Cut the music. Let's take a ten minute break."

The other girl had fallen, sprawling on her side on the polished wooden floors. Yuki dropped into a crouch beside her. "I'm sorry, again. Here, let me help you up."

The other girl looked up, her blonde ponytail swinging behind her. "Thank you. I'm grand though, really. No harm done."

Yuki stared at her. "You're Irish! Do you know how much I love an Irish accent? I think we're going to be great friends."

The injured girl giggled, sitting up straight. "If you say so. I'm Sinead. Good to meet you." Sinead took Yuki's hand, and scrambled to her feet. Then she smoothed down her uniform and straightened up to show off perfect posture.

"I'm Yuki. It's good to meet you too, Sinead." Yuki tipped her head to one side, studying Sinead. She seemed to be full of confidence. "Have you been with the airline for a while?"

Sinead nodded, her pale blue eyes striking. "A few years. I said I'd help train some of you new recruits. Be a mentor if you like."

Yuki straightened her own dress, not as elegant as the proper uniform. She couldn't wait to try it on. But who knew if she'd even pass the exams? She dropped her voice so the other trainees didn't overhear her. "I'd love for you to be my mentor. I think I'll need the help."

Sinead smiled, and she looked genuinely kind. "Do you want to grab a coffee with me? We can have a chat. The cafe downstairs is pretty good."

Yuki nodded, and followed Sinead towards the training room door. Sinead seemed like someone who would be a good friend. Yuki may not know much about emergency procedures or how to make sure the overhead compartments were secure, not yet. But she knew people, and often had a sense of what they were thinking. Working in the hotel had taught her that at least.

Yuki's phone buzzed in her jacket pocket, as they headed into the corridor. "Oh, I wonder who could be texting me..." She grabbed her phone and read the message. It was Declan.

**Declan:** *I'm heading to London for a few days. Be there Friday. :)*

She was no doubt grinning like a kid on Christmas morning, because Sinead asked, "Was that your boyfriend?"

She shrugged, playing it cool. "It's very new, but I really like him."

Sinead's lips tipped up at the corners, then she sighed. "Good for you. I should be so lucky."

Yuki stopped walking to read Declan's next message.

**Declan:** *Miss you, Miss Yuki.*

She replied, before she got too excited thinking about the weekend coming up. She wouldn't be able to concentrate if she let her imagination run wild.

**Yuki:** *Miss you too. Bring me a present from Ireland! Pretty please?*

**Declan:** *Since you asked so nicely, pretty girl. Call you later.*

**Yuki:** *xxx*

Sinead spoke, as they started walking again. "Are you still up for coffee?"

Yuki nodded. "Yes. I'm up for anything."

As she walked, Yuki's mind whirled. Maybe the thing between her and Declan would work out, even with them both working and travelling all the time. She hoped so.

She pressed her fingertips to the stunning necklace Declan had hidden under her tiny Christmas tree, before he left for Dublin. It was a swirly silver heart, from Tiffany's. She loved it. She hoped he liked the deluxe Santa hat and red silk tie she had couriered to his parents' house.

The new year was turning out to be an amazing ride so far. Her life of adventure had officially begun. Hopefully soon she'd be travelling the world, having adventures she'd couldn't even imagine yet.

Sinead winked at her, as she showed Yuki into the elevator, pretending to demonstrate the way to the emergency exits. "Let's go, Mermaid crew."

Mermaid crew. Yuki liked the sound of that. A lot.

# Thanks to...

Thanks to my family, and especially my superhero husband, for telling me I absolutely could write a novella and get it ready to publish by Christmas (even though I started writing it in November). He also agreed that a conga-line of Santas was awesome and definitely not too silly. You can see why I love him!

I'd like to thank my fabulous writing group, the Melbourne Romance Writers

Guild, for inspiring me and continuing to offer support, excellent advice and cups of coffee/snacks at our monthly meetings. In 2020 our writing group couldn't happen face-to-face, but we continued to chat online and honestly it was one of the bright spots of 2020 for me, including a hard lockdown for months where I live in Melbourne, Australia.

And thank you to my readers. It's been a long gap between book releases for me, mostly because of health issues. But I've enjoyed writing this novella and the indie publishing journey and hope to complete more stories before too long.

**2022 update:** A print edition is a little something I wanted to do in 2020 but I totally ran out of time. I hope some of my readers who prefer paperbacks enjoy it.

Thanks for reading!

# About Cassandra O'Leary

Cassandra O'Leary is an author,
avid reader, corporate communications
escapee, and film and TV fangirl.

In 2015, Cassandra won the global
We Heart New Talent contest run by
HarperCollins UK, and her debut novel,

*Girl on a Plane*, was published in 2016. Cassandra has also independently published several titles including *Hot In The City: A Romantic Comedy Story Collection*, all while chasing her two mini ninjas around her home city of Melbourne, Australia.

She is a proud member of Romance Writers of Australia, the Australian Society of Authors and the Melbourne Romance Writers Guild.

Read more at **cassandraolearyauthor.com** and sign-up for my newsletter for updates!

# Read next...

## Heart Note: A Christmas Romcom Novella

**A** laugh-out-loud Christmas novella, perfect for fans of *Love Actually* . . .

*Reviewers love Heart Note!*

"Someone call Richard Curtis, because *Heart Note* would make for a perfect holiday movie." –**Bookish Jottings**

"What a lovely book! It was romantic, festive fun with a little mystery thrown in."
– **Writing On The Wall**

"Lighthearted, amusing and delightfully festive!" – **What's Better Than Books**

"5☆ A Sexy, Saucy, Romantic Christmas read with a sprinkle of Mystery!" – **Dash Fan Reviews**

# Excerpt of Heart Note

## Two weeks ago…

**"I** can't do it." I blinked and eyed the crowd seated before me. There was no need for me to be up here on a platform in front of them. All their eyes on me.

*I don't want to do it. Please don't make me.*

They were all staring at me. I ran my sweaty hands down my skirt, sneaky style. But I didn't want to draw attention to my hips. I hugged myself around the waist.

"Of course you can do it. Do I have a volunteer?" The mean-eyed corporate trainer with the beaky nose and badly fitting navy suit shrugged and let out a shrill laugh. "Trust. It's crucial in a team environment." She scanned the crowd looking for willing victims. No such luck.

Beaky woman piped up again. "If I don't have a volunteer, Lily here will fail the assessment. She won't be able to start her new job."

"I don't mind, really. I'll do something else." Anything else. A new job even. No worries...

"Come on, people. I'm sure someone can catch her. She's not *that* fat." The horrible woman cackled.

*Oh. My. God.*

Boiling hot shame roiled through my belly and I bit my lip, hoping to slide right through the floor and into a parallel universe.

And then it happened. Just like something out of a movie. He stood up in the middle of the rows of seats, all the new staff around him staring with expressions ranging from mild interest to obvious relief.

I was nervous enough already, now he had to volunteer to help me like some sort of overly handsome dark knight to my damsel in distress. I was no damsel, but in distress? Check!

He moved into the aisle and began a slow, silent march to the front of the room where I stood.

*If I fell, would he catch me?*

*Would I want him to let go?*

*Would I be too heavy and crash straight through his arms and onto the floor like a baby elephant?*

Questions raced through my mind as I stood tall and concentrated hard on a square air-vent on the far wall, with two evenly spaced steel bolts and a long line underneath. If I squinted, it almost looked like a smiley face. But I didn't want to look all squinty. What if he took one look at my squinty face and sat down again?

I glanced at him quickly, so as not to look like I was looking. But I was. He'd made his way almost to the front of the room.

Oh no. He was coming this way. What was his name? I couldn't remember. We'd all introduced ourselves briefly in a horrible 'getting to know you' game a few days ago, but it was a blur.

He was so good-looking my tongue had gone all thick and rubbery. I couldn't remember my own name. But his was Chris...something.

*Christos!* That's right.

I stood on the podium in front of a room full of fresh-faced new retail staff, half perky and excited, half bored out of their gourds, staring at me as if I was a museum exhibit. Only Christos volunteered to help me. He volunteered to *catch* me. He sauntered towards my spot at the front of the room. My knees quaked. For real.

Christos. A gorgeous Greek-god-like name for a gorgeous Greek-god-like man. Or a fallen angel, some sort of demigod. Or part demon maybe. I shook my head, the fanciful ideas getting in the way of the important work of real-life ogling. Today he was wearing a fine black wool sweater and dark denim jeans, which hugged some truly impressive thighs. I don't know when

I'd ever been impressed by a man's thighs before, but I was now. Mightily.

And I was staring with intent. I wouldn't have had to spell out my intent, if it came to the point. I'm sure my goo-goo eyes conveyed the message, loud and clear.

I remembered now, he would be a security officer at the same store where I was going to work. I snapped my eyes upwards before he arrested me for most likely illegal thoughts about a colleague... Not helping my distractedness. I could have dealt with Christos snapping handcuffs on my wrists.

*Yes, sir.*

He sauntered some more, coming right up to the baby-poo-brown carpet square in front of the podium, and me. Only about thirty centimetres separated us, but honestly it felt like less. A beat of my heart, no more.

"Hi." He said the short word with a depth of feeling and throatiness, leaving me temporarily speechless. His eyes were so dark. Penetrating. "Are you all right?"

I nodded, furiously, so as not to give the wrong idea. The wrong idea being that I didn't want him to catch me.

The trainer, who I'd momentarily forgotten even existed, cleared her throat. "Right! Are we ready? As I was saying, trust is super important between team members. This exercise is a great bonding activity!"

I don't know why the woman was so excited about corporate training, but she was just so damned perky, or evil, I wasn't sure which. I didn't know whether to laugh or vomit. I settled for swallowing hard, ignoring the dry-throat syndrome Christos induced.

He raised one eyebrow and quirked the corner of his mouth, sending me into a head spin I didn't quite recover from before he spoke. "Turn around."

*Whoosh!* My underwear went up in flames.

Okay, not quite, but I was worried the smoke alarm on the ceiling would go off. I did enjoy being bossed around by the right man.

I turned on the podium so my back was to him. Suddenly, my spidey sense tingled. Or maybe it was my pheromones sparking with his. He was so close behind me I could feel his body heat emanating towards me, massaging the back of my neck. Or it could have been his fingers. Oh! It was his fingers.

And his scent...honeyed cinnamon and lemongrass wrapped around my olfactory gland and made it very happy indeed. A good-looking and a good-smelling man—a rare and delicious combination.

With a tap on my shoulder, he rumbled, "I'm right behind you." His hands were gone. A whoosh of cool air followed.

This was it.

Crunch time.

I had to trust Christos.

I had to fall.

I closed my eyes, scrunching my eyelids tight so not even a sliver of light got past them. I let my head tip back. My body dropped low and lax, my knees bent, my heart pounded in my ears. And I pushed off.

I fell.

Into his arms.

His strong, reliable arms were wrapped around my waist. His chest was pressed to my back and oh, yes. He had me. But I was possibly having a heart attack.

"My heart," I said, and he smiled. Perfectly straight white teeth flashed at me, while some kind of rampantly handsome smile lines danced on his face.

*Dazzling. Dazzled. Dazed?*

Whatever the proper word for what I was feeling, I was in a kerfuffle. Understatement of the millennium.

"I'm here," he mumbled, only for my ears. "Trust me."

*Oh, hubba hubba.*

Something warm and lovely swelled under my breasts. Maybe this job wouldn't be so bad after all.

**Buy now to continue reading: books2read.com/HeartNote**

# Also by Cassandra O'Leary

Hot In The City: A Romantic Comedy Story
Collection
Heart Note: A Christmas Romcom Novella
Friday I'm In Love: A Sweet and Saucy
Romcom Novelette

*Chocolate Truffle Kiss: A Romantic Comedy Novelette*
*Tree Love: A Romantic Short Story*

## Where to find my books

Please visit my website at
**cassandraolearyauthor.com/books**